Closed Legs Don't Get Fed

Reds Johnson

Closed Legs Don't Get Fed
Copyright © 2015 by Reds Johnson
Interior Design Formatting | Strawberry Publications, LLC

ISBN-13: 978-1718808379
ISBN-10: 1718808372

.

One

It was pouring rain outside as Chelsea ran to the nearest phone booth. She fumbled around in her purse until she found two quarters and nibbled on her fingernails as she waited for the person on the other end to pick up.

"Hello, Jason? I need a ride. I'm on 6th Street in Vineland. Look, I'm sorry about the other night, but I really need you right now," she begged.

"It's fine, I'm glad you called. I'm on my way. Don't go anywhere," Jason replied before ending the call.

Chelsea waited inside the phone booth until Jason got there. About twenty-five minutes later, she saw his 2012 gray BMW pull up. Jason hopped out of the car and ran over to Chelsea, holding a blanket.

"*Come on*," Jason yelled as he put the blanket around her and ran her to the passenger side door.

Once Chelsea was safe and sound inside the car, he got in and pulled off.

"What were you doing out there this time of night? It's pouring down raining," Jason asked.

"Look, that's not important, but thank you for coming to get me," said Chelsea.

Jason shook his head in disappointment. He already knew why Chelsea was out at this hour. He tried his best to get her off of the streets, but she wouldn't listen.

"Why are you shaking your head?" she asked.

"Because, Chelsea, why won't you let me help you? I mean, I've known you for six years and not once have I judged you, so please let me help," he begged.

Chelsea shook her head *no*. She knew Jason loved her, but she knew deep down inside that she was not wife material. Chelsea was twenty-six years old and was a prostitute. She could never keep a stable job or home, so she turned to the streets at the age of twenty-one and never looked back. She appreciated everything that Jason had done for her, but she knew deep down inside that she would only bring pain and drama to his life.

"At least stay at my place for the night. You can take a shower and put on some dry clothes, and you will have a warm bed to sleep in tonight," Jason said.

"Ok, fine. I'll stay the night, but I'm leaving first thing in the morning," Chelsea responded.

Jason was relieved. Several minutes later they pulled up to his house and got out. Once they were inside, Chelsea caught chills. Jason's house was beautiful. It was so cozy and warm to her.

"You can go upstairs and take a hot shower. I'll whip up something, considering it's too late to order anything. The towels are in the closet, and my bedroom is the second door on the left. You can go in there and put on one of my shirts and a pair of my briefs," he explained.

"Thank you," she responded as she made her way upstairs.

Chelsea peeked her head in each of the four rooms upstairs. She was very pleased by what she saw. The two rooms on the right were the guest rooms and the bathroom, and the other two rooms on the left were Jason's room and the computer room. She went inside the bathroom and turned on the shower. Chelsea looked in the mirror and touched her face.

Her pale white skin held a few red bruises on it, but she was still very beautiful. Her bright green and blue eyes were something that kept anyone's attention. Chelsea stood at 5'6" and weighed at least 165 pounds. She pulled out her hair tie and quickly combed the tangles out of her long blonde hair. She managed to smile, but it quickly turned into a frown when the chipped tooth in her mouth appeared. A few nights ago a guy she was giving oral sex to punched her after she realized he had paid her with fake money.

Chelsea had thought about going to the police, but she knew that they would look at her as if she was some sort of joke, so she dealt with it on her own. She got in the shower and let the hot water run all over her body. Afterwards, she grabbed her washrag and soap and began to wash up. Once she was done, she got out and grabbed a towel.

Chelsea didn't bother to dry her hair; she just left it as is. She headed to Jason's bedroom and closed the door. After searching through his dresser, she finally found his shirts and quickly dried off so she could put one on. As Chelsea was about to walk out of the room, she saw Jason's wallet sitting on the nightstand. She walked over and picked it up.

"I'm sorry, Jason," she said, barely above a whisper.

Chelsea opened his wallet and pulled out two fifty dollar bills. She put the wallet back and grabbed her dirty clothes and purse. As she came down the stairs, she smelled grilled food.

"Jason, what are you doing?" she asked.

Jason did a double take when he heard Chelsea's voice. Even though she had on one of his oversized shirts, he could still see her curvy figure.

"You look so beautiful," he said.

Chelsea blushed.

"Oh, stop it. Now tell me what you're doing," she said.

"Well, I had some steaks thawing out for tomorrow, but I said hey, why not cook them up now? So, I have prepared some grilled steaks and asparagus, along with some grilled corn on the cob and a nice side salad," Jason explained as he showed his pearly whites.

Chelsea couldn't help but smile. Jason was such a sweet guy, and she sometimes wished she was in a position to be with him. Not only was he sweet, but he was such a handsome guy, standing 6'2" with the skin complexion of vanilla bean ice cream. Jason had a slender frame and bright blue eyes, along with a nerdy look. He wore his light brown hair in a spikey style, and no matter where he was he always had a pencil tucked behind his ear.

"Wow. Well, thank you for preparing all of this, but could you give me a bag for my dirty clothes?" she said.

"Sure," Jason said as he grabbed a small bag out of his pantry and handed it to her.

"Thank you," Chelsea responded as she put her clothes in the bag and tied it.

"Well, the plates are fixed, so let's sit down and enjoy this wonderful meal," Jason said proudly.

Chelsea put her bag down and sat at the table. She really hadn't eaten anything in the last few days, so she began to chow down on the food. Jason watched in awe as she took a big forkful of salad and steak. Chelsea felt a bit embarrassed.

"I'm sorry. I've just been so busy, I guess I forgot to eat this morning," she lied.

Chelsea was always on the streets, and with the little bit of money she did make, she spent it on her bad drug habit. Jason knew Chelsea all too well, which is why he always tried to make her feel as comfortable as possible.

"No, it's fine. I'm glad you're enjoying your meal," he said.

For the next hour or so, they ate dinner and made small talk. Chelsea figured she should turn down because it was getting late, and because Jason was starting to ask personal questions. She was ashamed because she knew Jason saw a light in her that no one else saw.

Chelsea sometimes wished that Jason treated her like everyone else did. The fact that he knew she sold her body for money and sometimes drugs and yet still loved her made no sense. Chelsea didn't have time for love because she was all about chasing a dollar to get by day after day.

"You can sleep in the guest room for the night, because I know you don't want to sleep with me," Jason said.

"Yes, the guest room is fine, Jason. Goodnight," Chelsea said as she went in the room and closed the door.

Jason went inside his bedroom and stripped down to his briefs. He sat on the bed, took the pencil from behind his ear, and placed it on the nightstand. Jason noticed his wallet was moved. He picked it up and opened it, quickly noticing he was missing one hundred dollars. Jason felt uneasy. He was hoping Chelsea didn't steal from him and he had misplaced the money somewhere.

He erased the thought, placed his wallet back on the nightstand, and lay down. As Jason lay there, staring up at the ceiling, he thought about Chelsea and what it would take for her to be his. He knew the lifestyle Chelsea lived, but he loved her dearly, and all he wanted to do was help her. He always thought that someday she would just stop giving her body to unknown men and just be his, but that was just wishful thinking.

Two

Chelsea woke up kind of late the next morning. She hopped up out of the bed and ran downstairs. The smell of French toast filled the air, which made her stomach growl. When she walked into the kitchen, she saw Jason sitting down reading the paper and drinking a cup of coffee. He didn't give her much eye contact when he spoke.

"It's almost the afternoon. I didn't think you were the type to sleep this late," he said.

Chelsea didn't know if Jason was taking a cheap shot or not, so she ignored it.

"How are you?" she asked as she rubbed the sleep out of her eyes.

"I'm fine. Breakfast is on the stove," Jason said dryly.

Chelsea went to the stove and grabbed a slice of French toast. She poured herself a cup of coffee and sat at the table. Jason gave her no conversation at all.

Chelsea wasn't used to seeing Jason act this way. After she was done with her breakfast and coffee, she got up.

"Well, I think I should be going now. Thank you for everything, Jason," she said.

"You're welcome. Your bag is by the door," Jason said without looking up.

Chelsea was hoping he would volunteer to drop her off somewhere, but he didn't. She walked to the door and noticed she had a different color bag. She quickly picked it up and opened it. Chelsea noticed her clothing was now clean and the two fifty dollar bills were now gone. She put on her jeans from the night before and began searching her bag. Jason heard her rummaging through the bag and got up.

"Are you looking for this?" Jason said while holding the two fifty dollar bills.

Chelsea looked stunned. She knew that Jason washed her clothes while she was asleep and found the money she had taken from him. Her best bet was to try to play it off.

"Actually, yes. I was looking for that. I dropped some money out of my purse last night and I put it in my bag. Thank you for finding it," Chelsea explained as she walked over and tried to take the money

Jason couldn't believe how she was lying right to his face. He was so hurt because he thought Chelsea cared about him way more than that.

"You are full of so much bullshit, Chelsea. I checked my wallet last night and noticed I was missing 100 dollars, and then this morning I'm trying to be generous and wash your clothes and look what I find. How could you do this to me, Chelsea?" Jason said.

Chelsea looked at him, her eyes now light blue. She was getting angry at Jason.

"How could I do what to you, huh? I told you not to put your all into me, and you did anyway, Jason. You know how I am. You invited me into your house, so whatever happened while I was here is all on you," Chelsea snapped.

Jason was shocked by her response, and it showed all in his face.

"You know something, Chelsea? I thought that you would let me help you. I thought that you would realize that the love I had for you all these years is still there, but I guess not, so if this money is so important to you, then take it," Jason said as he held the money out.

Chelsea walked over and snatched the money out of Jason's hand and headed for the door.

"Chelsea," Jason called out.

She stood there with her back turned to him and her hand on the knob.

"What, Jason?" she answered.

"Just tell me one thing, and then you can go," he said.

"What do you want to know?" she said.

"Was it worth it? I mean, was stealing from me really worth it? All you had to do was ask. You knew I would have given you the money," he emotionally stated.

"Yes, it was worth it. What you fail to realize is that you're fully established, Jason, and I'm still scraping from the bottom of the barrel. I'd rather steal from you than ask you and have you question me about why I need the money. I'm trying to make sure I live to survive the next day," Chelsea responded and then walked out.

Jason stood there, lost for words by her response. He didn't understand why she was so cold toward him. Chelsea walked down the street, letting the afternoon breeze hit her. She tried to forget about Jason and the incident. She walked a few more blocks until she made it to a bus stop. As she sat there and waited, a teenage guy came and sat next to her. Chelsea could feel his eyes on her.

"Excuse me, is there something you want?" she said.

"I'm just tryna figure out why a beautiful snow bunny like you out here at the bus stop. Where yo' man at, baby?" said the guy.

Chelsea couldn't believe the nerve of this guy. He didn't look a day over eighteen and had the nerve to be talking to her like she was some high school groupie.

"I'm single, and the name isn't snow bunny. It's Chelsea," she replied.

"A'ight, well, I'm Derrick. Where you on ya way to?" he asked.

"To a friend's house," she lied.

"Well look, I'm 'bout to go to the crib and smoke some Kush. You can come through if you want," Derrick said.

Chelsea thought on it for a moment. She didn't mind smoking a blunt right now, because she needed it. She was use to going with strangers, so this situation was no different.

"Ok, I'm down," she agreed.

"Cool. Well, we can get off on ma stop," Derrick said as the bus pulled up.

They both got on the bus and took a seat. Through the whole ride Derrick was smiling at Chelsea. At first it didn't bother her, but now it was making her feel funny.

"Why are you smiling at me?" she asked.

"Because you so damn beautiful," he responded.

"Well, thank you, but I would appreciate it if you don't smile at me like I'm the last dinner roll on the table," Chelsea told him.

Derrick couldn't help but to laugh.

"Ma bad," he told her.

Chelsea checked her surroundings and realized they were still in Vineland. She was now a lot more comfortable because she knew where she was going, and she would know her way back. Derrick pushed the stop button.

"You live here?" she asked.

14

"On the next block," Derrick responded as he got up.

They both made their way off the bus and proceeded to walk to Derrick's house. When they finally made it there, Chelsea was pleased to see he didn't live in any projects. Derrick reached into his pocket, took out his keys and unlocked the door.

"Welcome," he said as he walked in.

"This is nice. You live by yourself?" she questioned.

"Nah, ma momma, but she forever at work," Derrick replied.

Chelsea looked around while Derrick went into the kitchen. He came back out with two bottled waters.

"Oh thank you. And your father doesn't live with you?" Chelsea grabbed the water.

"No problem, and nah, fuck that fiend. Come on, we can go to ma room," he told her.

Chelsea didn't respond after he said that. She followed Derrick upstairs to his bedroom. When they got there, he began stripping down to his undershirt and boxers. Derrick went to his dresser and grabbed a wrap and a little bag of weed.

"You can sit down, baby, don't be nervous," he told her.

Chelsea put her things down and sat on Derrick's bed. She watched him roll the blunt as if he was a pro.

"How old are you?" she asked.

Derrick smiled and looked at her.

"How old I look?" he asked.

Chelsea studied him for a second. He had golden brown skin with big doe eyes. She knew he couldn't be no older than eighteen. However, he was very handsome, and even though she got nervous when he smiled, that was one of his best features. Derrick was about the same height as Chelsea. That was pretty much the only thing that turned her off.

"I'm 21," Derrick told her.

Chelsea was surprised. She knew he had to be lying.

"Let me see some ID?" she said.

Derrick burst into laughter.

"You dead ass or nah?" he asked.

"I'm dead serious," Chelsea responded.

Derrick reached into his pants' pocket, pulled out his wallet and took out his ID.

"See, I'm 21, girl," he said as he handed it to her.

Chelsea examined it to make sure it wasn't a fake ID, and it wasn't. She didn't understand why a twenty-one-year-old would still be living with his mother, but she was in no place to judge.

"Wow, I really thought you were, like, 17 or 18," she told him.

"Yeah, I get that a lot," Derrick said as he lit up the blunt and took a couple of pulls before passing it to Chelsea.

She pulled long and hard and held the smoke in before exhaling. That instantly made Derrick's dick hard, the way she pulled on the blunt. He moved a little closer to her on the bed and began rubbing on her titties. Chelsea pushed him away and looked at him.

"What are you doing?" she asked.

"Ma bad, baby, you just got ma dick hard as hell right now," said Derrick.

"Nothing in this world is free, baby," Chelsea told him.

Derrick looked at her hoping she was joking, but she wasn't.

"So, you mean to tell me that I gotta pay for the pussy?" he asked.

"Yes, that's exactly what I am telling you," Chelsea said as she took another pull of the blunt.

"Look, I ain't never paid for pussy a day in my life, and I ain't 'bout to start now, so how about we just smoke and fuck, and I got a few homeboys that can pay you some big money for that thang," Derrick told her.

"How do I know that you're not full of bullshit? Because I don't play when it comes to my money" Chelsea said sternly.

Derrick threw his hands up in defense.

"Look, baby, I ain't on no bullshit, especially when it's about making money. Now, help me and I'll help you," Derrick said as he pulled out his rock hard dick.

Chelsea eyes nearly popped out by the sight of Derrick's dick. She wondered how someone so small could carry such a big package. She passed the blunt back to Derrick and grabbed his nine-inch monster. It was so thick that her hand couldn't fit around the whole thing. She twirled her tongue around the tip of his dick and massaged his balls at the same time.

"Damn, girl," Derrick moaned.

After he said that, Chelsea went in for the kill. She swallowed him whole and began gurgling on his dick. She sucked him hard, and then she sucked him slowly as she stroked his shaft. Chelsea then began jerking Derrick off as she hummed on his balls, and that drove him crazy.

"Damn, baby, let me see what that pussy do," said Derrick.

Chelsea got off of the bed and took off all of her clothing. She climbed on top of Derrick and slid down until all nine inches of him was inside her. Chelsea ground her hips back and forth just enough to get her juices flowing. Derrick grabbed her hips and pushed himself in and out of her. Chelsea played with her nipples while she rode him.

"You like this white pussy, don't you?" she asked flirtatiously.

"Hell yeah! You like this black dick in that white pussy?" Derrick asked back.

"Yes, daddy, I want you to slam that dick in and out of this pussy nice and hard," she said.

"Oh, shit, then get up and turn around so I can beat that shit from the back," Derrick told her.

Chelsea did exactly that. She bent over and let Derrick enter her from behind. He pushed her back down so her back could be arched more. Derrick began pounding Chelsea hard, just how she wanted it.

"Just like that, right?" he said.

"Yes, just like that!" Chelsea screamed.

Derrick grabbed her hips and pounded her nice and hard as his balls made a loud slapping sound.

"Aw, fuck!" he moaned.

The harder Derrick pounded her, the more she slammed back into him. He could tell she was enjoying it, so he decided to take advantage of it. He began rubbing her asshole as he pounded her pussy. After a while he slid his thumb in her ass.

"Oh my gosh, Derrick," she moaned and then jumped.

"Relax, baby," Derrick told her as he played in her ass with his thumb.

Once she was open enough, he pulled his cum-covered dick out of her pussy and began pushing it into her ass slowly.

"Yeah, I'ma fuck this snow bunny ass nice and hard," Derrick said as he watched his thick dick disappear in her ass.

Chelsea had a tight grip on his pillow as she felt Derrick's dick moving in and out of her. Derrick wasted no time. He started pounding away.

"Yeah, take that dick, take it," he said.

Chelsea was in pain, but she was accustomed to being treated that way during sex. Derrick reached down underneath her and began playing in her pussy as he fucked her in the ass. Now Chelsea was enjoying it. She actually wanted more.

"This feels so good," she moaned.

Derrick lay on top of her, causing her to lay flat on her stomach. Chelsea felt every inch of him. Derrick felt he was about to cum, but he didn't want to do it before her, so he started playing with her clit faster and faster.

"Oh, I'm going to cum, Derrick! Stop! Oh my…. I'm going to cum right now," Chelsea moaned, but that didn't stop Derrick.

He slow pumped her as he played with her clit. Chelsea was trying to stop Derrick, but he pinned her hands above her head.

"Ooooh, I'm coming," she moaned out loud.

Derrick started pounding her hard and fast and continued to play with her clit. Chelsea's body was going crazy. She was experiencing pleasure and pain. Before she knew it, she was squirting all over his bed and hand, and yet he kept going.

"Derrick, I'm coming!" she screamed loudly.

"Mmmmmm, shit! Oh shit," Derrick moaned as he released his warm load inside of Chelsea's ass.

He pulled out, and Chelsea had cum oozing out of her gaping hole.

"Damn, that shit was good, baby" Derrick told her as he smacked her on her sore ass.

"I'm glad you enjoyed yourself," she responded.

"Hell yeah. You can go shower, if you want," he said.

Chelsea slowly got off of the bed and grabbed her clothes.

"Thank you. Where is your bathroom?" she asked.

"Second door on the left everything you need is in there already. Ma mom keep everything stocked up," he told her as he lit up another blunt.

Chelsea made her way to the bathroom. When she got in, she sat on the toilet and began pushing Derrick's nut out of her. Afterward, she grabbed a clean washcloth and washed herself thoroughly. Chelsea dried off, put her clothing back on and went back to Derrick's room.

"So, when are you going to call your boys?" she said.

"I figure you might want to get ya'self together before I call them," he responded.

"Ok, that's fine," she told him.

"How old are you?" he asked.

"I'm 26, why do you ask?" she said.

"I was just wondering, no biggie," he shrugged his shoulders.

Three

As the day went on and Chelsea saw it was getting late, she grabbed her purse and was about to leave.

"Look, it's getting late. I have to go," she told him.

"My boys on their way now," Derrick told her.

"If you're bullshitting me, I'm leaving," she told him.

"Baby, ain't nobody bullshitting you," Derrick said.

Chelsea sat down and waited. She wondered if they were going to try to rape her. She looked around Derrick's bedroom for a weapon that was in arms reach. Derrick noticed her getting nervous.

"Relax, baby, ain't shit gon' happen to you," he told her.

Chelsea tried to trust him, but she trusted no man. A little while later, she heard a knock on the door. Derrick went downstairs to answer the door.

Chelsea then heard more than one person coming up the stairs. When Derrick entered the room again, a total of eight guys followed.

"Chelsea, this ma niggas Dirk, Montae, Dog, Man, Eazy, Dontrae, Spree Well, and Cruz," Derrick introduced them.

"Nice to meet you all," she said.

Some nodded and some rubbed their hands together as if they were getting ready to eat a hot meal.

"Chelsea, how you wanna do this? Because these niggas got dough," Derrick said.

"Gangbangs are 500 and up. If you all want me one on one, then 100 dollars an hour," Chelsea stated with folded arms.

They all could tell that Chelsea was about a dollar.

"Damn, it don't take me long to nut," Eazy spoke up.

"Ok, then 50 for you minute, man," Chelsea shot back.

Everyone burst into laughter.

"Well, ma mom working a double tonight, so y'all go ahead and get it in. I'ma sit back, smoke, and watch some TV," Derrick told them.

"Where are we going to do this at?" she asked.

"It's a guest room down the hall, baby," Derrick told her.

Chelsea got up and grabbed Eazy and walked out of the room. She could tell that his sex game was going to be whack just by the way he walked. When they entered the guest room, Chelsea pushed Eazy on the bed.

"Pay up," she told him.

Eazy reached into his pocket and pulled out 50 dollars.

"I'll pay you after I get pleased," he told her.

"No, you pay now or get the fuck out and let the next guy come in," Chelsea said with attitude.

Eazy shook his head and handed her the fifty dollar bill. She stuffed it in her purse, got on her knees and proceeded to unbuckle his pants. She pulled out his soft dick and began jerking him off. Chelsea stopped in mid-stroke, got up and quickly took off her jeans.

"What position do you want to do?" she asked.

"Shit, a nigga like me fucks with doggy style," Eazy said with pride.

Chelsea laughed in her head. She climbed back on the bed and bent over. Eazy got behind her and slid his six-inch dick inside her. He started pounding away like a rabbit. Chelsea didn't moan, not once.

"*Fuck,*" Eazy yelled as he released all over her ass.

Chelsea grabbed an empty pillowcase and wiped off her ass.

"That was good," he told her.

"You can send in Dirk" Chelsea told him, not fazed by his compliment.

Eazy walked out of the room like he was the man. When he walked into Derrick's room, all eyes were on him.

"How was it, tho'?" Montae asked.

"I told y'all she was a good fuck. Shorty about a dollar. I can't knock her for using what she got to get paid," Derrick said.

"It was good, but Montae, she want you next," Eazy pointed at him.

"Yo, Spree Well, Cruz, and Dog, we running up in that together, right?" Montae asked.

"Hell yeah," they responded at the same time.

"I just want some head from shawty," Man chimed in.

27

"Yeah, I'm wit that," Dontrae agreed.

When all four of the men entered the room, Chelsea was surprised.

"Here is 150," Montae said as he handed her the money.

"Y'all want a gangbang, I need my 500 right now. If you all go past an hour, I'm going to need another 500," she told them.

They all handed her their cut and started to take off their clothes. Chelsea couldn't wait until this was over. The first one up was Montae. He started kissing and sucking on her nipples. Spree Well walked over with his dick in his hand. Chelsea started sucking on Spree Well while she jerked off Montae with the other hand.

"Yeah, girl, just like that," Spree Well moaned.

Chelsea switched and started sucking Montae's dick. Cruz and Dog just sat there and watched.

"Fuck y'all just standing there for? Y'all niggas betta come get y'all money's worth," Spree Well barked.

They both walked over to the semi-circle, and Chelsea gave all four of them the best head they ever had. She pushed Montae on the bed and climbed on top of him and began riding him viciously.

"Ride that shit," Montae said as Chelsea bounced up and down on him.

Spree Well mounted her from behind and slid his dick inside her ass. They both double penetrated her as she licked and sucked Dog and Cruz's dicks.

"*Fuck me,*" she yelled.

Spree Well choked her from behind as he pounded her harder.

"Fuck, I'm 'bouta cum," Spree Well said.

He then released inside of her and pulled out. Dog got behind her and rammed his dick inside of her ass and began pumping her quickly. As they pinned her down, Montae gently bit on her nipples. The headboard was slamming into the wall as they sexed Chelsea in all three of her holes.

"Mmm, oh fuck," Montae moaned as he released inside her.

Dog started to push in and out of her slowly with his eyes closed. He reached for her boobs and grabbed them both roughly as he slammed down hard three times.

"Oh fuck," Chelsea moaned.

"Urgh," he moaned as he busted inside of her.

Montae pushed her on the bed and got up. As she lay on her back, Cruz climbed on top of her and began sucking on her neck and he went deep inside of her. He gave her slow deep strokes and kissed her passionately.

"Look at this nigga tryna make love and shit," Montae laughed.

"Y'all niggas done, now get the fuck out and let me enjoy mines," he huffed.

They all got dressed and let out of the room laughing. Chelsea's body was tired. She was glad that Cruz decided to go slow, but she really just wanted him to get finished so he could get off of her.

"Come on, baby, go faster," she begged.

"I wanna take my time," he told her.

Chelsea wrapped her legs around his back and stuck her tongue in his mouth.

"No, I want you to pound this pussy better than your homeboys did," she told him.

Cruz looked at her and then kissed her again. He grabbed the headboard and started fucking Chelsea hard like she wanted it.

"Yes! Oh, fuck me harder, baby, harder," she moaned.

As Cruz fucked her, the bed hit the wall harder and harder, which made the room shake. Chelsea couldn't wait to get her money and get out of that house.

"Ooh, fuck," Cruz moaned.

He pulled out of Chelsea and wiped the last of himself on her. He got off of the bed and got dressed.

"That was pretty good," he told her.

Chelsea didn't respond. She quickly put on her clothes and grabbed her purse. She didn't bother to say goodbye to Derrick. She just made her way out of the house.

Four

Over the next few weeks, Chelsea felt her body going through a change. She didn't know what was going on with her, but she didn't like it. She sat in the Days Inn throwing up nonstop.

"What is going on with me?" she said to herself.

She got up and brushed her teeth. When she looked in the mirror, she burst into tears. Chelsea knew this could only mean one thing. She was pregnant, and she had no clue who the father could be. Chelsea grabbed her purse and went to the front desk to use the phone. She dialed Jason's number and waited for him to pick up.

"Hello," he answered.

"Hey, Jason, how are you?" she asked.

"Hello, Chelsea, and I'm fine. How are you?" he said.

"I'm fine. I wanted to know if you could come get me. I'm at the Days Inn. Look, I'm really sorry about what I did. Can I make it up by taking you out to dinner tonight?" she asked.

Jason's heart filled with joy. He finally felt like he was getting somewhere, and he wasn't going to miss this opportunity.

"Sure, I'll be there," he said as he hung up.

Chelsea went back to her room and gathered her belongings. She knew what she was about to do was wrong, but at this point she didn't care. She was in no place to raise a child, so she had to put her plan into action. About thirty minutes later, Chelsea heard a horn outside. When she peeked out, she saw Jason's car. She grabbed her things and left.

"Hey, let me get that for you," Jason said as he grabbed her bags.

"Thank you, sweetie," Chelsea said.

They got into the car and headed to Jason's house. Chelsea looked over at him.

"I thought I said I would take you out to dinner."

"I know, but after I got off the phone with you I was so excited I couldn't help myself, so I have some spaghetti cooking right as we speak," Jason said as he showed all 32 pearly whites.

"You are too much," Chelsea said as she rubbed the side of his face gently.

When they got to his house and Chelsea walked up to the door, she could smell the aroma of the food. Jason could put his foot in a meal, and that was something Chelsea loved about him.

"Smells good, doesn't it?" Jason asked as he unlocked the door and welcomed her in.

"Yes, it smells lovely," Chelsea replied.

Jason grabbed her bags and took them upstairs for her. He felt in his heart that Chelsea was finally going to be with him, so he wanted everything to be special. He ran a nice hot bubble bath for the both of them. Jason headed back downstairs to check on dinner.

"I hope you don't think I went through a lot of trouble preparing this meal. It was nothing, really," Jason told her.

"You wouldn't tell me if you did go through trouble making this," Chelsea said with a chuckle.

Jason grabbed a bottle of wine and poured two glassed. Chelsea was going to decline, but she couldn't. She had to go along with her plan.

"Thank you," she told him.

"You're welcome, my love," said Jason.

"This is absolutely amazing," Chelsea said as she watched Jason place the food on the table.

"Anything for you," he told her.

As they ate and talked, Jason debated whether he should ask her if she was done with the streets, but he thought it either now or never?

"Chelsea, I'm just going to be straight up and forward with you. I love you, and I always have. I don't care what you have done in the past. I want us to be together and have a family. I want you to be my wife," Jason blurted.

Chelsea was stunned. She knew he loved her, but she had no idea that he wanted her to be his wife. She didn't respond right away.

"I-I don't know what to say, Jason. This is all so sudden," she told him.

"Say that you're done with the streets and that you will be my wife," he told her.

She took a brief moment before responding.

"Ok, Jason, I will be you wife," Chelsea said.

Jason jumped up and ran over to her. He picked her up and kissed her deeply.

"Thank you, Chelsea. All I ever wanted was a chance," he said excitedly.

Chelsea smiled, not because of the happy moment they were having, but because she only agreed to be his wife, not leave the streets.

Five

Chelsea was seven and a half months pregnant, and Jason was happy to soon be a father. He proposed to her, and they were now engaged. Jason was the happiest man alive. He finally had the girl of his dreams, and he planned to do anything to keep her happy.

"You are so beautiful," Jason said when he walked in the bedroom.

Chelsea was getting dressed when he walked in. She hated being pregnant, but if this was what she had to do in order to make it to the top, then so be it, she thought.

"Thank you, Mr. Hardy," she said and then gave him a peck on the lips.

"You're welcome, soon-to-be Mrs. Hardy. It feels so good to finally be able to say that I've known you for six long years, and the wait was definitely worth it," Jason said.

Chelsea smiled, but that smile quickly turned into a frown once she felt a sharp pain in her stomach.

"*Ouch!*" she yelled.

"Chelsea, what's wrong? Are you ok?" Jason asked in concern.

"No, my stomach hurts," she told him.

Without hesitation, Jason grabbed his keys and picked her up.

"Jason, what are you doing?" she asked.

"I'm taking you to the hospital," he told her.

They made it out to the car and he put her in. Jason was nervous and excited because Chelsea may have been in labor. Although she was in pain, Chelsea was happy that this was almost over. They got to Vineland hospital and he rushed her in.

"My wife is in labor," he yelled.

"We need a wheelchair," a nurse yelled.

"Sir, how far along are the contractions?" the nurse asked.

"I'm not sure. She's only seven and a half months. I think she may be having the baby early," he responded.

"We need to get her in the delivery room now. She's going into an early labor," said the nurse.

They all ran back into the delivery room, and Jason was right there. Once they were in the delivery room, they got Chelsea in her hospital gown. When Jason went to change into his scrubs, he heard Chelsea screaming, and then he heard cries.

"It's a girl," the doctor said out loud.

Jason ran back into the room with the nurse. He walked over to Chelsea's bedside and kissed her.

"How did this happen? I didn't even get a chance to see my child born," Jason said with his head low.

"It's ok, Jason. You're here now," she told him.

They laid the baby on Chelsea's chest after she was cleaned and weighed. Chelsea could finally go on with her life now that she was no longer pregnant. She knew that she was in labor, but she never said anything. Chelsea had been drinking a cap full of castor oil every day for the last week. She had no intentions on ever keeping the baby.

Six

It had been a week since Chelsea had the baby. Jason was sound asleep when he heard the baby crying. As the crying went on and on, he got up and looked around.

"*Chelsea*," he called out.

She didn't answer. Jason quickly went into the baby's room. He picked up baby Chelsea and grabbed her pacifier and put it in her mouth. He searched the house, but Chelsea was nowhere in sight. When he went into the kitchen, there was a note on the table. He opened it and saw that it was from Chelsea.

> *Jason,*
>
> *By the time you read this letter, you will realize that I am long gone. Thank you for everything. You were the only man who truly loved me for me. I'm sorry to say that I'm just not*

the wife type. I have a few things to confess. My first confession is that seven and a half months ago you told me to tell you that I will leave the streets and be your wife, but I only agreed to be your wife, not leave the streets. My second confession is that I was already pregnant that night you came to pick me up from the Days Inn. And Jason, my last confession is that I used this marriage for money. Once I got your bank information, I made a separate account that I've been transferring money to from your account. Sorry, Jason. I love you, but this is just how the game goes sometimes. Please don't give up on little Chelsea because of my mistakes. Take care of her for me.

Love,

Chelsea.

A single tear fell from Jason's face once he finished the letter. He couldn't believe that Chelsea not only used him, but left him to raise a baby that wasn't even his. Jason was crushed. He didn't know what he would do or how he would act if he ever saw Chelsea again.

Seven

Tears rolled down her face as she arrived in Germantown, Philadelphia. She felt terrible for what she had done, but she was glad that she could start a new life without any responsibilities. Her bank account was full, and she couldn't wait to party.

Chelsea chose to move to Philadelphia because it was fast paced. The streets never slept, and in her eyes that meant that money was always going to be made. When she pulled into her two-story house, Chelsea felt amazing. She knew that she had done a lot of wrong to get where she was at, but to her it was all worth it.

She had been on her own selling her body since she was 21 years old. Her parents disowned her after they found out what she was doing. They thought their plans for her were very simple. Graduate high school, go to college, and become a doctor. Chelsea didn't want that. She wanted to plan her own life and make her own decisions.

After selling her body for so long and receiving nothing but pennies for it, she was finally getting somewhere and would do everything in her power to keep it that way. She parked her car and got out and embraced the man who was waiting for her with open arms.

"You finally made it," Derrick said as he grabbed her bags from her.

"Yes, it was a long drive, but well worth it. This house is amazing, by the way," Chelsea responded.

"It is, and I'm glad I took you up on your offer," Derrick said as they headed into the house.

After Chelsea had her daughter, she called Derrick and wanted to see if they could do business together. She respected Derrick because he respected her and her lifestyle. He didn't judge her about the way she got her money, and that was all she needed to see. Chelsea decided not to mention the baby, because she didn't want to scare Derrick away knowing that it was a strong possibility that one of his friends was the father.

"Well, this is the beginning to a new life for the both of us. Let's celebrate," Chelsea said as she went to the kitchen and grabbed two beers out of the refrigerator.

She gave one to Derrick and they cheered. Chelsea gulped half of hers down while Derrick only took a few sips. He stared at her for what seemed like forever. Derrick saw Chelsea as a moneymaker, and nothing more. After what his boys told him, he knew he could score big with being her pimp, and that's exactly what he intended on being.

Eight

"How much money did you make from the club tonight?" Derrick asked.

"Fifteen hundred," Chelsea said proudly.

"Ok, give me five hundred and you keep the rest," Derrick said as he scrolled through his phone.

Chelsea peeled off five one hundred dollar bills and handed them to Derrick. Business was going great, and Chelsea had no complaints, considering Derrick let her keep most of the profits.

"I know you tired. Go get some sleep," he told her.

"I figured we'd watch a movie and spend a little time together, since I've been working since I got here" Chelsea explained.

"I gotta get up early tomorrow, and so do you, so that's why I said get some sleep," Derrick said without looking up.

Chelsea stood there for a brief moment before turning around and walking upstairs. She went into the bedroom that she and Derrick shared and took off her clothes. After putting on her robe, she got into bed. It had been a long night, and as she sank deeper into the silk sheets, she realized how tired she really was.

Nine

The next morning, Chelsea was woken by her nipples being nibbled on. She though it was Derrick, but when she opened her eyes she was surprised by a fat white man and his bald head. Before she could get a word out, he had spread her legs and roughly forced himself inside of her. Chelsea gasped, not because of his length, but because of the thickness the man carried. He quickly pounded away at her already sore vagina from the night before. All she could do was wait until the moment was over.

The man was sweaty and he smelled of musk. She realized that this was the busy day Derrick was referring to.

"Oh, your pussy is so tight, baby," the man moaned.

Chelsea was truly disgusted. She'd had some terrible sex partners in her time. She even had sex with a few crack addicts, but this was by far the worse sexual experience she has ever had. Chelsea wanted it to end quickly, so she tightened up her vaginal walls and wrapped her legs around the man tightly, causing him to dig deeper and deeper inside of her.

"Fuck, I'm going to cum in this warm pussy. Oh god, oh god, here it comes!" He moaned as he released inside of Chelsea.

Her face frowned as he pulled himself out of her. He stuck two fingers inside of her pussy and began to move in and out of her slowly. Chelsea pushed him back.

"Are you finished yet?" she asked in a disgusted tone.

"Not yet. Not until I taste what I've put inside of you," he told her.

Chelsea didn't understand at first. That was until he put his face between her legs and proceeded to suck forcefully.

"This is awful," Chelsea said out loud.

When the man came up, he had a yellow film around his mouth. He smiled a crooked smile that made Chelsea's stomach turn.

"You were worth every bit of that four grand," he said as he got up.

Chelsea sat up and closed her legs. She waited until the man got dressed and left before she got up. She ran downstairs in her housecoat searching for Derrick, who was sitting in the kitchen sipping on a cup of coffee.

"You bastard! How dare you invade my privacy that way?" she spat.

Derrick looked up and smiled.

"Well, look who's finally awake. I hope you enjoyed your good morning gift," Derrick said as he pushed two grand across the table.

Chelsea looked at the money and then back at Derrick.

"How could you send that stinky, fat fuck in there while I was asleep?" she snapped.

"His hygiene ain't have shit to do with me. The only thing that concerned me was that four grand he was giving up," Derrick told her.

"Well, next time you need to do a hygiene check on the guys you send me," Chelsea said as she grabbed the money off of the table and then stormed upstairs.

She could hear Derrick chuckling downstairs, which made her even angrier.

Ten

Chelsea was sitting at the bar, helping herself to back-to-back shots. It was 12:00 a.m. and the night was extremely slow at the Purple Orchid. She made about four hundred dollars alone. She lit up a cigarette and took a long pull before putting it down.

"Hello, beautiful," a guy greeted as he took a seat next to her at the bar.

Chelsea looked over at the tall dark and handsome man in the black pin-striped suit. She was a bit impressed at how clean his attire was. She picked up her cigarette and pulled on it before blowing the smoke in his face.

"Hello," she said in an uninterested tone.

The man waved the smoke out of his face before continuing.

"I'm Jeremy, and you are?" he asked.

"Chelsea. Nice to meet you, Jeremy," she said as she extended her hand.

"The pleasure is all mine. So, what is a lovely lady like you doing here?" he asked.

"I work here. Is that a problem?" she asked.

Jeremy looked Chelsea up and down before responding.

"Not at all, but how about we go somewhere so we can get a little bit more acquainted?" Jeremy insisted.

Chelsea looked at him, and his whole body read dollar signs.

Anything is better than being here tonight, she thought to herself.

"Sure, let's go," she agreed as she put out her cigarette.

Jeremy took Chelsea by the hand and led her outside of the club to his 1986 Cadillac Deville. Chelsea could tell by the way he dressed and by what he drove that he was an older guy. He opened the passenger side door for Chelsea and she got in.

"How old are you?" she asked when Jeremy got in.

"45. Why, am I too old for you?" he said with a smile.

Chelsea applauded him for taking care of himself. He looked damn good to be a 45-year-old man, and she didn't mind at all because she was tired of dealing with younger men.

"No, you are just right," she said with a smile.

As they drove, Chelsea noticed that he lived in the area as well. She wondered why she never saw him around and decided to ask.

"So, how come I've never seen you around before?" she asked.

"Well, I'm originally from New York, but I'm just down here doing business," Jeremy explained.

"Oh, ok. What kind of business do you do, if you don't mind me asking," Chelsea wanted to know.

"No, it's not a problem. And I own a car dealership in New York. I'm looking to expand my business here," Jeremy explained.

"Oh, ok. That sounds nice," said Chelsea.

As they pulled up to a beautiful townhouse, Chelsea smiled.

So far so good, she thought to herself.

Jeremy got out and opened the passenger side door for Chelsea. When they got in the house, it seemed as though he was already expecting to have company tonight. There was a bottle of wine on ice and two wine glasses sitting on his living room table.

"Looks like you were expecting to have a good night," Chelsea said.

"Well, I knew I was going to meet a beautiful woman tonight, so I decided to make sure things were prepared for both me and her," Jeremy said as he took of his jacket.

They both took a seat on the couch and he poured himself and Chelsea a glass of wine.

"From what I can see, you have a beautiful house," she said.

"Thank you. All I'm looking for is my queen to share it with," he said flirtatiously.

That was an instant turn off for Chelsea. She was in no way, shape, or form looking to be in any type of relationship. She was about her money, and if it wasn't about money, then it didn't concern her.

"Well, I appreciate the wine, but I should be getting home," she said as she proceeded to get up.

Jeremy gently grabbed her arm. He could tell by his comment that she was no longer interested, so he made his next move.

"How about we unwind a little?" Jeremy said as he pulled out a crack pipe and a bag filled with what looked like rocks.

"What's the catch?" she asked.

"Nothing, let's just enjoy the moment," he said.

He filled the pipe with two rocks and grabbed a lighter. As he lit it up, he sucked on it hard and held in the smoke before exhaling it. Jeremy handed the pipe to Chelsea, and she did the same. The night went on, and they were both high as a kite.

Eleven

When Chelsea woke up, it was around 2:00 p.m. and her cell was going off. She looked over and saw that Jeremy was still knocked out. She quickly grabbed her cell and looked at her missed calls. They were all from Derrick, and by reading the text messages she could tell he was pissed. Chelsea jumped up and put on her shoes. Jeremy was awakened by all the noise she was making.

"What's going on?" he asked.

"I have to get home. My boyfriend is worried," she told him.

A frown appeared on Jeremy's face when she mentioned the word *boyfriend*.

"What the hell do you mean, boyfriend? You ain't say shit about a boyfriend last night," Jeremy said with a scowl on his face.

Trying to recap what happened last night, Chelsea really had no clue. All she remembered was coming back to his place and sipping wine. Everything else was a blur.

"Yes, I have a boyfriend. And you never asked, so that's why I never mentioned it, but look, I have to go," she said as she headed downstairs.

"Fucking white trash! Get the hell out of here," Jeremy yelled in anger.

Chelsea laughed inside. She couldn't believe how angry he got when she mentioned that she had a boyfriend. Jeremy was acting like a lunatic, and she didn't have the time to deal with that.

Twelve

When Chelsea got home, Derrick was sitting at the kitchen table, furious.

"Hey, baby. Sorry about all of this, I..." was all Chelsea could get out before she went flying back across the kitchen.

Derrick looked as if he was possessed with the way he kept beating on Chelsea. He kicked, stomped, and pulled her hair. Chelsea's body was in excruciating pain. Derrick had completely lost his mind.

"Don't you ever fuckin' make me miss out on money, bitch!" he yelled.

"I — I'm sorry," she slurred.

"Get the fuck up and clean yo'self up. We got money to make," Derrick snapped.

Chelsea slowly got up. She held onto the rail as she made her way upstairs. Her head was throbbing and her body ached. When she went into the bathroom and looked into the mirror, she cringed at the sight of her face. Chelsea broke down crying. She didn't expect Derrick to get so violent with her. She got a clean white washcloth and wet it with hot water. Chelsea gently cleaned the blood off of her face. She didn't know why, but an image of her daughter Chelsea popped up in her head. She shook it off and continued to get cleaned and changed.

"*Chelsea, are you ready?*" Derrick yelled upstairs.

"*Yeah, I'm coming down now,*" Chelsea yelled back.

"*No need. Stay right there,*" Derrick told her.

Chelsea did as she was told. She sat down on the bed as she heard footsteps coming up the stairs. She looked to the door and was greeted by a skinny male who looked no older than fifteen. He wore an oversized shirt and baggy jeans that were halfway down his butt. His nappy dreads were all over the place, and it looked as if he hadn't bathed in days.

"Whaddup, shawty?" he said as he dragged out each word.

Chelsea could tell that the young boy wasn't from around here. By the way that he dressed, she figured maybe he was visiting from somewhere.

"How old are you?" she asked.

"I got a big dick, shawty, so that's all that matters," he responded.

Chelsea rolled her eyes in disgust. Derrick was really overstepping his boundaries with the men he was sending her.

"What's your name?" Chelsea asked.

The young boy dropped his pants and exposed his long dick.

He wasn't lying. Chelsea thought to herself.

He began stroking his dick, and Chelsea watched as he became fully erect. He was long and thick, and the veins in his dick were bulging out. Chelsea could tell he needed to release.

"I'm not really in the mood for all the talkin', shawty. I came here for one thing, and one thing only, so either you give it to me or I'ma take it," he told her.

Chelsea stripped out of her clothing and walked over to the boy. When she grabbed his penis, he shook his head no.

"Nah, bend over on the edge of the bed," he told her.

Chelsea did as she was told and walked over to the bed. She bent over and arched her back as much as she could. He smacked her ass hard a few times and she winced a little. He spread her ass cheeks apart and spit between them. Before Chelsea could say anything, she felt a burning sensation as the boy penetrated her ass.

"*Oh my gosh!*" Chelsea screamed.

He forcefully pounded away as Chelsea screamed in pain.

"*Please stop it! This hurts,*" she begged.

"Fuck that, I paid money for this ass, and you gon' shut the fuck up and take it," he barked.

He grabbed a fistful of her hair and rammed harder and harder. All Chelsea could do was deal with what he was giving her. She thought Derrick cared for her, but as time went on she realized he didn't. After a while she stopped screaming and pleading. The only sounds were the bed slamming against the wall and his balls slapping against her pussy.

Thirteen

"I told you, daddy gon' take good care of you," Jeremy said.

Chelsea sat in the corner of his bedroom, smiling wildly. She put the crack pipe to her mouth and lit it up again. As she inhaled deeply, her body became numb all over again. She watched as Jeremy sat on the edge of the bed and put the poison into his veins.

"Come here," he slurred.

Chelsea crawled over to him and he pulled his pants down. Jeremy was twelve inches, but he held no thickness at all. He shoved his dick in her mouth and she began sucking it like her life depended on it. Chelsea felt like she was flying. All the pain she felt from the beating Derrick gave her the other day was gone.

"Let me take another hit, baby," Chelsea said as she stopped and got up.

Jeremy stood up and slapped Chelsea.

"Bitch, I didn't tell you to stop. Get back on your knees," he snapped.

Chelsea's face burned and turned red. It was like déjà vu all over again. She did as she was told and got back down on her knees and continued sucking.

"Yeah, baby, just like that," he moaned.

Chelsea bobbed her head up and down quickly. She wanted Jeremy to release so she could get her next hit. Jeremy held onto her head and pushed it down with force. Chelsea gagged, which turned Jeremy on more.

"Urgh, fuck," Jeremy growled as he released inside of Chelsea's mouth.

She swallowed every drop of him and then stood up.

"Daddy, can I please get a taste now?" she begged.

Jeremy laughed as he watched her beg for another hit.

"How bad do you want it?" he asked.

"Real bad. Please, daddy, don't make me beg any longer," she said.

Jeremy grabbed the crack pipe and set it up for her. He held it out, but then snatched it back when she reached for it.

"Lick daddy's ass, and then you can have a taste," he told her.

Chelsea's scratched her tangled hair as she eyed the pipe greedily. As of now, she didn't care. She was willing to do anything to get her next hit. Jeremy laid back, lifted his legs up, and parted his ass cheeks. Chelsea got down and hungrily licked and sucked Jeremy's ass, all while eyeing her glass pipe.

Fourteen

Jason looked in the mirror at the dark rings around his eyes. Between work and baby Chelsea, he barely got any sleep. He prayed night after night that Chelsea would come to her senses and come back, but so far he had no luck. After Chelsea left, Jason took it upon himself to get a DNA test for their daughter, and Chelsea was right. The baby wasn't his.

Even though he already knew, it still hurt him to know she went through all of this just to get money from him. He didn't understand why she slept with men when she knew he would give her the world.

"Jason, where do you keep the formula?" Mary asked.

After Chelsea left Jason high and dry to take care of their newborn baby, he called his mother, Mary, to help out. Chelsea took every dime he had out of his bank account. She left him with nothing. Jason had to move out of his four-bedroom house into a one-bedroom until he could afford something bigger. Baby Chelsea took the room while he slept on the living room couch.

"Check the cabinets, mom," he replied dryly.

"Ok, I found it. Come on out here and sit with me," she told him.

Jason threw some cold water on his face and then grabbed a towel to dry it. He took his time as he walked out of the bathroom and into the kitchen.

"I can't believe all of this happened to me. I mean, after all I've done for her, this is the thanks I get," Jason said.

"Now Jason, I told you she was bad news from the start, and the first thing you need to do is look into an adoption agency so you can give this baby up," Mary said in disgust.

Jason looked at his mother as if she had something ugly on her face.

"What do you mean, *this baby*? And how dare you tell me to give up baby Chelsea? Mother, have you lost your mind?" Jason asked.

"You, sir, are the one who has lost their mind. Taking care of this nigger baby here. This child is a demon, and you need to get rid of it," Mary said as she rocked the baby violently.

Jason stood up and took baby Chelsea out of his mother's arms. He took her to the room and laid her down gently. When he came back out, his face was beet red from anger.

"How dare you say something like that about my daughter? I don't give a damn if she was blue. That is still my daughter, so you can take that negative shit elsewhere," Jason snapped.

Mary looked stunned by his outburst. She stood up and grabbed her purse before speaking.

"You raise your voice at me over a child that isn't even yours, Jason?" Mary said.

"She is my child. She is my daughter whether you like it or not. We may not have the same bloodline, but I will not love her any less just because her mother done me wrong, and I would like for you to leave," Jason said as he went to the door.

Mary looked as if she wanted to cry. When she got to the door, she looked into Jason's eyes.

"All I wanted was the best for you, but you decided to run after the trash. Now look at you," Mary said and then walked out.

Jason slammed the door behind her. He went to the couch and sat down. It had been a long day, and all he wanted to do was rest. Jason was so full of emotions. He didn't know what his next move would be, but he knew he needed to make one fast.

Fifteen

"**S**tupid bitch. You constantly fuckin' with ma money. What, you think this a fuckin' game?" Derrick spat.

He dragged Chelsea by her hair up the stairs. Her back burned from the scrapes and bruises caused by the staircase.

"I'm sorry. I'll pay you back, Derrick," she pleaded.

"Nah, fuck that. You gettin' high with ma shit, you fuckin whore? Don't use ma muthafuckin' money to support ya habit," Derrick said as he kicked her repeatedly in her stomach.

Chelsea was in fetal position in the middle of the bedroom floor, bleeding from the mouth and nose. Derrick had found out that she had been getting high and she was using his money to do it.

"I'ma show you, bitch. When I tell you don't fuck with ma money, I mean that shit," Derrick said as he unbuckled his leather belt.

"Derrick, baby, I will work it off. I promise," Chelsea said as tears ran down her face.

"Get up and get in the fuckin' bathroom," Derrick ordered with a scowl on his face.

Chelsea slowly got up and went into the bathroom. Derrick pushed her into the shower, and she landed with a hard thud. He turned on the shower and began beating Chelsea with his leather belt. Chelsea's screams could be heard miles away. Welts appeared everywhere on her body as the hot water hit her and Derrick beat her with his belt. The only thing that was on Chelsea's mind was getting a hit so she could no longer feel the pain.

Sixteen

I t'd been two weeks since the horrible beating Chelsea got from Derrick. She sat on the porch with nothing but a white tee shirt on. Not only was her body sore, but so was her pussy and ass. Derrick was making her pay back every dime with interest. Derrick had ordered her to do gangbangs and sex parties. Chelsea no longer felt human. She wanted out because she was no longer getting paid, she was just being used and abused.

"Chelsea, get the fuck in here," Derrick said with anger.

Her body was shivering cold when he opened the door for her. Chelsea quickly got up and went inside.

"Look, Friday night you got a big date, so go douche or whatever you gotta do to get that pussy tight and right, because this nigga giving up 10 grand," Derrick boasted.

Chelsea's eyes lit up. Since she'd been supporting her habit, a lot of the money she took from Jason was being spent on that, and this was just what she needed.

"Thank you, daddy," Chelsea said as she smiled big.

"Yeah, you know I always try to look out for you. Now, if you really wanna thank me, you need to get on ya knees and put that mouth to work," Derrick said as he undid his jeans.

Chelsea got on her knees and put Derrick in her mouth. She instantly started deep throating him and slobbering on his dick.

"Yeah, just like that," he moaned.

Chelsea palmed his balls and gave them a gentle squeeze as she twirled her tongue around the head of his dick. Derrick lay back with his eyes closed as Chelsea went to work on his Johnson.

Seventeen

After thinking about what he would do as far as baby Chelsea, Jason had finally come to a decision. He took out a $100,000 loan from the bank and bought a mini condo for himself and baby Chelsea. Jason hired an old friend of his to babysit Chelsea while he worked. He wanted Chelsea to have nothing but the best, and he was going to work hard giving it to her. He still prayed for her mother, but his only focus was his daughter. Jason finally realized that he had to move on and stop living in the past. Since he met Chelsea, he put his all into helping her, and he got burned in the process. Jason looked at it as a lesson learned.

You can't save someone who doesn't want to be saved, he thought.

Eighteen

She stood on the corner dressed in nothing but a floor-length mink coat with a pair of black stilettos. Chelsea pulled out a cigarette and lit it up as she waited for her date. Derrick sat in the car and waited until the guy pulled up to pay him.

"Damn, bitch, put that fuckin' cigarette out," said Derrick.

"Oh, fuck off, Derrick. I ain't bothering you," Chelsea shot back.

"Actually, you is. I don't need this muthafucka thinking of any reason to pay us any less," Derrick told her.

Chelsea rolled her eyes and flicked her cigarette into the street. Just then, a silver Cadillac pulled up. Chelsea expected more, but she didn't speak on it. The door opened, and out stepped Jeremy. Right then and there Chelsea felt uneasy. She was trying to get rid of Jeremy because he was starting to catch feelings for her, and she didn't have time for that.

She knew if Derrick found out she was having relations with Jeremy it would be some serious problems. Chelsea didn't know how Jeremy found out about Derrick, but he did, and he was using this situation to his advantage. When he came up to Chelsea, he was smiling from ear to ear, but it wasn't a happy smile. It had danger written all over it.

"Enough of all that meet and greet shit. Where ma money at?" Derrick asked.

Jeremy went over to the driver's side window and gave Derrick a bag. When Derrick opened it, his eyes lit up in excitement. He ran his hands through the neatly stacked cash.

"A'ight, y'all two have a good time. Chelsea, I'll be waiting here at 2:00 a.m. on the dot," he said sternly.

"Ok, daddy," Chelsea said as she blew him a kiss.

Derrick pulled off without looking back.

"Well, well, well. So, we meet again," Jeremy said.

"Look, let's just get this over with," Chelsea said as she got inside the car.

Jeremy followed and got inside the car as well. As they drove, Chelsea felt very uncomfortable. She didn't understand why, because this wasn't the first time she had been with Jeremy, but for some reason things just weren't the same. They pulled up to a restaurant, and Chelsea felt better once she was around people. They went inside and took their seats as their waiter came over.

"Order whatever you want," he told her.

"I'll just have a glass of wine and a salad," she told the waiter.

"I'll have the steak dinner," Jeremy said.

The waiter took their orders and walked away.

"Why are you acting so strange?" Chelsea asked.

Jeremy sipped his water before speaking.

"To be real, I'm still upset about you just using me to get high. I could've done way more for you than that wannabe pimp you're with," Jeremy told her.

Chelsea laughed loudly.

"You could never do more for me than what Derrick has already done," Chelsea said with confidence.

Jeremy's jaw got tight and Chelsea noticed it, so she tensed up a little.

"You know what? It's cool," he told her.

"I have to go to the ladies' room," Chelsea said as she got up and grabbed her purse.

When she made it to the ladies' room, she took out her cell and called Derrick.

"What the fuck you doing calling me when you supposed to be fuckin' and suckin'?" he told her.

"This guy is making me feel uncomfortable. Can you please cut the date short?" Chelsea begged.

Derrick blew loudly into the phone. *Fuck it, I already got ma money,* he thought.

"A'ight, cool. Cut that shit short," he told her.

"Thank you, daddy," Chelsea said and then ended the call.

When she got back out, her food and wine was at the table. Jeremy was sitting there patiently waiting.

"Sorry about that. Derrick called to let me know the date has to be cut short," Chelsea said as she gulped down her glass of wine.

"I paid ten fuckin' grand to be with you. Fuck that," Jeremy barked.

"Well, that's not my problem. Daddy's rules are daddy's rules. Now, can you please take me back?" Chelsea said as she headed to the door.

Jeremy was fuming. He hands were shaking and his palms were sweaty. He took out a little plastic baggy that contained a white, powdery substance. Jeremy then took his pinky fingernail, got some out and snorted it up each nostril. He cracked his knuckles and swiped everything off of the table and walked out. Everyone looked shocked by what he just did. Jeremy got into the car and slammed the door hard.

"You wanna be with this nigga, then cool," Jeremy said as he sped off.

"You need to slow down. I can't believe you're acting like this," Chelsea said.

Jeremy sped in and out of traffic. His mind was in a thousand places at once. He was seeing three of everything. Everything seemed to be moving all at once. Jeremy was starting to hear voices, so he began banging on his head with his fist.

"Get the fuck out of my head," he yelled.

"Pull over right now, Jeremy! Let me out of this damn car," Chelsea said in a frightened tone.

Jeremy ignored her and kept on going. He sped past a police car, and they put on their sirens and followed. Jeremy only stopped because he had reached his destination. Once he saw Derrick's car, the emotions started flowing and he became angry all over again. As Chelsea opened the car door and proceeded to get out, Jeremy grabbed a handful of her hair and slit her throat.

"If I can't have you, then nobody can," he yelled and then sped off just as the officer approached his door.

Derrick got out of the car, but hopped right back in and sped off once he saw the police. Chelsea was on the sidewalk, holding her neck and gurgling on her own blood. Her life was flashing before her eyes, and the last image she saw was of her daughter.

Nineteen

I t was Monday morning, and Jason was getting ready for work. He, Sarah, and baby Chelsea went away for the weekend to celebrate the fact that he had just landed a second good-paying job. Sarah was an old friend of his whom he had hired to babysit Chelsea while he went to work, and they were getting pretty close. After he was done getting dressed, he went downstairs to get some breakfast.

"That doesn't make any sense at all," Sarah said as she shook her head at the TV.

Jason wrapped his arms around her petite frame and kissed her on the neck. Sarah was a true beauty. Her chocolate skin was smooth, and her light brown eyes were big and round. Her curly 'fro was big and full with a small flower in the front. She was 5'6", and everything about her read a true African queen.

"What's wrong, baby," Jason asked.

"Some lady named Chelsea White was left for dead in Philadelphia. Some guy slit her throat. They said she was a prostitute, but I don't care what she was. No one had the right to do that to her," Sarah shook her head in disgust.

Jason's heart dropped. As he looked at the screen, he saw all of this happened Friday night. He felt terrible, because while he was out celebrating, someone was harming Chelsea.

"What's wrong, sweetie?" she said.

"I know her," Jason said with his head low.

"Oh my gosh, is that Chelsea's mother?" Sarah asked.

"Yes, that's her. Chelsea has my last name, not her mother's, that's probably why you didn't notice. I feel terrible," Jason explained.

"Baby, I am so sorry that this happened. Why didn't you tell me about her mother? We could have tried to help her," Sarah said.

"No, Chelsea can't be helped. Believe me, I've tried. I've done all I could for her. I know this happened for a reason, but I have to get to work," Jason said as he got up.

He didn't quite know how to handle this situation. A part of him wanted to run to Chelsea's rescue, but then a part of him wanted to say *I told you so.* All in all, he knew he couldn't go to the hospital to see Chelsea, because that would just bring back old feeling he was trying to keep in the past. Jason did what he had been doing for Chelsea, which was pray for her.

Twenty

Derrick was in Palms Springs, living the life. His bank account was full, and he had ten grand in his pocket. After everything went down that night, he cleaned out Chelsea's bank account and got ghost. As far as Derrick knew, Chelsea was dead, and he wasn't trying to go down for any of that.

"Sir, would you like another drink?" the waitress in the bikini asked.

"Yeah, give me a long island iced tea," Derrick replied as he lit up his cigar.

In a way, Derrick felt bad for the way things went down between him and Chelsea. She wasn't a bad girl, she just got caught up in the wrong things. He took advantage of her because he needed the money, but what bothered him most was when he found out she had been dealing with his father, Jeremy.

He never respected Chelsea as a woman, but he respected her hustle for money. His father, Jeremy, was a crack head, and he knew whomever came in contact with him would fall victim as well. Derrick hated his father for influencing his mother to get on drugs. He started selling weed at the age of sixteen to make money to get his mother into a good rehab. Once she got clean, they moved and never looked back to their old life again.

"Here you go, sir," the waitress said as she sat down his drink.

"I can't get a happy ending?" Derrick asked.

The girl looked at him and smiled. She was average, but she had a beautiful bronze skin tone.

"You didn't even bother to take me my name," she said with a playful attitude.

"Oh, I'm sorry, gorgeous. I'm Derrick. What's your name?" he asked.

"Tiffany," she responded.

"Nice to meet you, Tiffany. Now, what about that happy ending?" Derrick said as he unzipped his pants.

Tiffany giggled as she went between his legs and got on her knees. Derrick eyed her as she grabbed ahold of his dick and took every last inch of him into her mouth.

"Damn, this is definitely paradise," Derrick said with a moan.

Twenty-One

I t'd been four months since Chelsea almost lost her life. After going through physical therapy and drug rehab, she was finally able to walk the streets again.

"Mrs. White, I wish the best for you. And remember, if you need anything, please don't hesitate to call," said one of the rehab workers.

"Thank you. I appreciate all you have done for me," Chelsea said with a smile as she walked away.

She got to the bus stop and smiled big as she looked around. It felt good to feel and smell the fresh air. Chelsea was clean and ready to live life the right way. She was ready to be with Jason and raise her daughter. She got on the bus and headed to her destination.

Twenty-Two

The bus ride was long, but peaceful, and it was just what Chelsea needed. She walked up to Jason's door and knocked twice. Her heart warmed when she heard baby Chelsea's cooing and talking. When the door opened, Chelsea was greeted by a black woman.

"Hello, may I help you?" Sarah asked.

"Yes, I'm here to see Jason," Chelsea responded.

"May I ask who you are?" she said.

"Tell him that it's Chelsea," she responded with more attitude than needed.

Sarah looked Chelsea up and down and then noticed a long cut across her neck. She couldn't believe she was actually staring Chelsea in the eyes.

"Please come in," Sarah told her.

Chelsea smiled and walked in. Jason's home was beautiful, and it gave her a warm feeling. It still felt very homey.

"*Honey, you have company,*" Sarah yelled.

When Chelsea heard that, she looked over at Sarah and gave her the evil eye. She was hoping her worst nightmare was not about to come true. Jason came out from the living room with baby Chelsea in his arms and froze in his footsteps.

"Hi, Jason. How are you?" Chelsea said.

"I'm — I'm fine, Chelsea. How are you?" he asked.

"Better. Much better," she told him.

"That's good to know," said Jason.

"Wow, she is getting big," Chelsea said as she walked over to Jason and her daughter.

"Yes, she is. And she's as healthy as ever," Jason said with a smile.

"Thank you for taking care of her. I feel horrible for leaving you two, but now I'm back, and I'm ready for us to be a family. Jason, I am ready to marry you," Chelsea said as she hugged him.

Sarah stood there looking for Jason to respond. She wasn't quite sure how she should've reacted. Chelsea realized Jason wasn't hugging her back, so she pulled away.

"What's wrong?" she said.

"Chelsea, I'm afraid it's too late for that now," Jason said.

Chelsea looked confused.

"What do you mean?" she asked.

"Chelsea, I'm engaged. Sarah is my fiancée," Jason revealed.

Chelsea's heart dropped. She couldn't believe what she was hearing. This was a smack in the face to her. She thought Jason would always be there waiting for her, but she was wrong.

"Wow. Jason, I thought we would be a family," Chelsea told him.

"Chelsea, sweetheart, I've tried. I have always tried to be there for you, but you pushed me away. You've done any and everything in your power to hurt me and use me. I finally found a little strength to get over it," Jason explained.

"You said you would always be there for me," Chelsea said as tears ran down her face.

"You're right, I did say that, and I will always be there for you, but I can't be with you, Chelsea. I'm sorry," said Jason.

Chelsea wiped her tears away. She knew this day would come, but she never believed that Jason had the guts to move on from her.

"What about Chelsea?" she asked.

"She is well taken care of, and you can come see her whenever you like. I will not keep you away from our daughter," he said.

Chelsea looked Jason in his eyes. She had lost a good man. Life was hitting her hard in every direction. After everything she had done to Jason, he did the one thing she asked him to, and that was to take care of baby Chelsea. Even though she didn't want to walk away, she knew it was best. Chelsea turned to Sarah, who was standing by the door.

"He's a good man. Don't make the same mistake I did and lose him," Chelsea told her as she walked to the door.

"Chelsea, it doesn't have to end like this," Jason called out to her.

"Yes, it does, Jason. I can no longer let my life be a burden on you, and I damn sure don't want to be a burden on my child. I want her to be a better woman than I am," Chelsea told him as she walked out.

She walked down the street to the bus stop. As she sat there and waited, a guy came and sat next to her. Chelsea held her head low so he wouldn't see the tears falling from her eyes.

"Excuse me, is there something you want?" she asked as she wiped her face.

"I'm just tryna figure out why a beautiful snow bunny like you out here at the bus stop alone. Where yo' man at, baby?" the guy asked her.

Chelsea looked up at the guy. It was déjà vu all over again, and before she knew it she was in his apartment, having sex with him and eight of his friends for money.

Twenty-Three

Jason sat at the kitchen table, holding baby Chelsea as he was deep in thought. Sarah came behind him and rubbed his shoulders.

"Baby, are you ok?" she asked.

"I wish I could say yes, but I can't. I didn't want things to end this way," Jason explained.

Sarah understood where Jason was coming from, but she also understood why Chelsea walked out the way she did.

"Jason, you can't keep beating yourself up over this. All things happen for a reason. Maybe Chelsea thought that this was best. I mean, you have to admit, us being together was probably a lot for her to take in" Sarah told him.

Jason held onto baby Chelsea as if his life depended on it. He felt like everything was falling apart once again.

"What do you mean by that?" Jason asked.

Sarah sat down at the table and looked Jason directly in the eyes.

"Jason, be honest. How many white women do you see come home and see their ex with a black woman? You don't hear about that often. It's always a black man leaving his black girlfriend or wife for a white woman. I just think this was all a bit much for her, and I can't blame her for feeling overwhelmed and walking out the way she did," Sarah explained.

Jason agreed. He didn't want to say anything, but he knew by the way Chelsea looked at Sarah that she was insulted. The only thing was, Jason didn't care because he loved Sarah. He loved the way she took care of baby Chelsea.

He loved the way she carried herself like the queen she was. Everything about her was like a breath of fresh air. When he was feeling down, she made sure by the end of the day he was wearing a smile on his face. Despite Chelsea walking out of his life again, Jason was happy. It took him a long time to realize that Chelsea didn't want to be helped, and he was now content with that.

He didn't lose Chelsea to drugs. Jason lost Chelsea to the streets.

Closed Legs Don't Get Fed 2
Available Now

One

"**S**orry about that. Derrick called to let me know the date has to be cut short," Chelsea said as she gulped down her glass of wine.

"I paid ten fuckin' grand to be with you. Fuck that," Jeremy barked.

"Well, that's not my problem. Daddy's rules are daddy's rules. Now, can you please take me back?" Chelsea said as she headed to the door.

Jeremy was fuming. His hands were shaking and his palms were sweaty. He took out a little plastic baggy that contained a white, powdery substance. Jeremy then took his pinky fingernail, got some out and snorted it up each nostril. He cracked his knuckles and swiped everything off of the table and walked out. Everyone looked shocked by what he just did. Jeremy got in the car and slammed the door hard.

"You wanna be with this nigga, then cool," Jeremy said as he sped off.

"You need to slow down. I can't believe you're acting like this," Chelsea said.

Jeremy sped in and out of traffic. His mind was in a thousand places at once. He was seeing three of everything. Everything seemed to be moving all at once. Jeremy was starting to hear voices, so he began banging on his head with his fist.

"Get the fuck out of my head," he yelled.

"Pull over right now, Jeremy. Let me out of this damn car," Chelsea said in a frightened tone.

Jeremy ignored her and kept on going. He sped past a police car and they put on their sirens and followed. Jeremy only stopped because he had reached his destination. Once he saw Derrick's car, the emotions started flowing and he became angry all over again. As Chelsea opened the car door and proceeded to get out, Jeremy grabbed a handful of her hair and slit her throat.

"If I can't have you, then nobody can!"

***

Jeremy couldn't take what he had done to Chelsea. Months went by and it was still eating him up inside. He never intended to hurt Chelsea, but he was so upset that she chose his son over him. In just a short period of time, Jeremy had fallen in love with Chelsea. He couldn't forgive himself for what he'd done. Jeremy knew that there was only one thing to do.

He sat in front of the Philadelphia Police Department and stared into space. Jeremy thought about how much wrong he had done in his life. After abandoning his son Derrick and his ex-wife Demetria, Jeremy used all of his life savings on drugs. He became a nobody, and that's just how his son treated him. Like he was nobody.

Jeremy got out of his 1986 Cadillac Deville. The walk into the police department seemed like an eternity to Jeremy. A policewoman behind the glass eyed Jeremy suspiciously. He walked over to the lady behind the glass and spoke with pride.

"My name is Jeremy Robinson, and I am turning myself in for the attempted murder of Chelsea White."

End of Excerpt

Reds Johnson also known as Anne Marie, is a twenty-three-year-old independent author born and raised in New Jersey. She started writing at the age of nine years old, and ever since then, writing has been her passion. Her inspirations were Danielle Santiago, and Wahida Clark. Once she came across their books; Reds pushed to get discovered around the age of thirteen going on fourteen.

To be such a young woman, the stories she wrote hit so close to home for many. She writes urban, romance, erotica, bbw, and teen stories and each book she penned is based on true events; whether she's been through it or witnessed it. After being homeless and watching her mother struggle for many years, Reds knew that it was time to strive harder. Her passion seeped through her pores so she knew that it was only a matter of time before someone gave her a chance.

Leaping head first into the industry and making more than a few mistakes; Reds now has the ability to take control of her writing career. She is on a new path to success and is aiming for bigger and better opportunities.

Visit my website www.iamredsjohnson.com

MORE TITLES BY REDS JOHNSON

SILVER PLATTER HOE 6 BOOK SERIES

HARMONY & CHAOS 6 BOOK SERIES

MORE TITLES BY REDS JOHNSON

NEVER TRUST A RATCHET BITCH 3 BOOK SERIES

TEEN BOOKS

A PROSTITUTE'S CONFESSIONS SERIES

CLOSED LEGS DON'T GET FED SERIES

MORE TITLES BY REDS JOHNSON

OTHER TITLES BY REDS JOHNSON

Made in the USA
Middletown, DE
08 July 2020